Dear Parent:

This story treats us to an important lesson: While surprises can be wonderful, they may also be problematic. If even the confident Clifford can begin to doubt that he is loved when his friends appear to be ignoring his birthday, any young child (and many adults, too) might react the same way.

But what is perhaps an even more important lesson is that it doesn't take much for young children to question whether or not they are loved. For one thing, it is developmentally normal for them to interpret things going on around them in a very personal way. Many a toddler or young preschooler has concluded that having just spilled his milk or her juice caused the clap of thunder or power failure that coincidentally followed. And while children may be familiar with the phrases, "Mommy is tired," or "Daddy is too busy to play," they often do not understand that those parental states are not their fault.

I can almost hear you sighing: "But if that's the case, how can we keep our kids confident and happy? We can't be ready to play every minute of the day." And of course, that is true. But it could help you to know what is behind your child's increasing demands for attention at those times when you can do the least about them.

In calmer moments, you may patiently sensitize children to others' needs and feelings, and guide them toward seeing the separateness of unrelated events. One wonderful way to do that is to read and talk about stories such as this one. Sharing *The Big Surprise* offers parents and children a chance to exchange ideas about Clifford's and his friends' mutual misunderstandings. It offers a relaxed opportunity to chat with children about believing in one's self and in the constancy of others' love.

Adele M. Brodkin, Ph.D.

Visit Clifford at scholastic.com/clifford

ISBN 0-439-22465-9

Copyright © 2001 Scholastic Entertainment Inc. All rights reserved.
Based on the CLIFFORD THE BIG RED DOG book series published by Scholastic Inc.
TM & © Norman Bridwell. SCHOLASTIC, CARTWHEEL BOOKS, and associated logos
are trademarks and/or registered trademarks of Scholastic Inc.
CLIFFORD, CLIFFORD THE BIG RED DOG, CLIFFORD & COMPANY, and associated logos
are trademarks and/or registered trademarks of Norman Bridwell.

Library of Congress Cataloging-in-Publication Data is available

10 9 8 7 6 5 4 3 2 1   01 02 03 04 05 06

Printed in the U.S.A.   24
First printing, September 2001

Clifford THE BIG RED DOG®

Scholastic

The Big Surprise

Adapted by David L. Harrison

Illustrated by Carolyn Bracken and Ken Edwards

**Based on the Scholastic book series
"Clifford The Big Red Dog"
by Norman Bridwell**

From the television script
"Clifford's Big Surprise" written by
Sheryl Scarborough and Kayte Kuche

SCHOLASTIC INC.
New York   Toronto   London   Auckland   Sydney   Mexico City
New Delhi   Hong Kong

"Emily ordered these balloons
For Clifford's special day."

"Pedro! Careful! Hang on tight!
You'll let them get away!"

"Victor! Pedro! Thanks for bringing
Clifford's big surprise!
Oh, no! Look who's spotted us!
Hurry! Hide them, guys!"

Emily! Emily! Hey! It's me!
Hey! It's you at last!
Now my birthday fun can start!
Now we'll have a blast!

"Clifford, try to understand
It's quite a busy day.
I've got to keep this crate . . .
    uh . . .
    warm!
That's why I can't play."

"Why don't you go find your friends?
They'll play with you, I know.
I promise later we'll have fun,
But now you need to go."

I wonder what I could have done.
I wonder if she's mad.
I wonder why she made me go.
Oh, I feel so sad!

"When Clifford sees his birthday bone
I bet his eyes will pop!
You think we'll get a little chew?"

"You're drooling, T-Bone! Stop!"

"T-Bone! Cleo! There you are!
Hey! Wait up for me!
Today's my birthday! Want to play?
Is that a bone I see?"

"Hide it, T-Bone! Hide it quick!"

"But, Cleo!"

"Shhh! Be still!

I'll give the wagon a little shove!"

"Okay, but we're on a hill."

"Hey! Hey! Hey! It's my big day!
T-Bone? Are you all right?"

"He swallowed an onion for his lunch!
His breath would turn you white!"

"I'm taking T-Bone home to brush!

We'll see you later on.

Psst! T-Bone, where's the wagon?"

"Psst, yourself! It's gone!"

"Dad, you made this birthday cake
Better than all the rest."

"Well, Clifford's quite a special guy.
He only deserves the best."

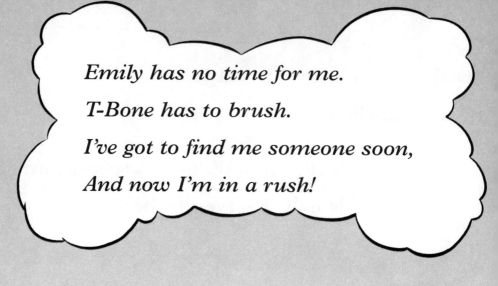

Emily has no time for me.

T-Bone has to brush.

I've got to find me someone soon,

And now I'm in a rush!

"Clifford's coming! Hide his cake!

Quick! Behind this tree!

Wow! He blew the icing off!"

"And blew it onto me!"

"Clifford?

Clifford!

Come home, boy!

Come on home to me!"

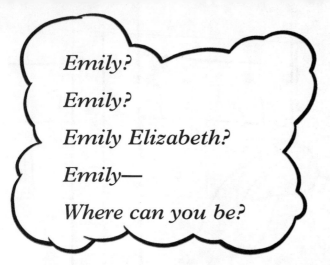

Emily?

Emily?

Emily Elizabeth?

Emily—

Where can you be?

"Come on, Clifford! Come on home!

You're going to miss the fun!

Run around the house and see!

Hurry, Clifford! Run!"

"Happy birthday, Clifford dear!
This is your surprise!"

It's Emily Elizabeth and all my friends!
I can't believe my eyes!

"We had to make up little fibs
And say we couldn't play!"

"But all of us could hardly wait
To celebrate your day!"

"We wanted you to be surprised
And never even guess!"

"So was it all worth
waiting for?"

"I think he's saying, 'Yes!'"

BOOKS IN THIS SERIES:

Welcome to Birdwell Island: Everyone on Birdwell Island thinks that Clifford is just too big! But when there's an emergency, Clifford The Big Red Dog teaches everyone to have respect—even for those who are different.

A Puppy to Love: Emily Elizabeth's birthday wish comes true: She gets a puppy to love! And with her love and kindness, Clifford The Small Red Puppy becomes Clifford The Big Red Dog!

The Big Sleep Over: Clifford has to spend his first night without Emily Elizabeth. When he has trouble falling asleep, his Birdwell Island friends work together to make sure that he—and everyone else—gets a good night's sleep.

No Dogs Allowed: No dogs in Birdwell Island Park? That's what Mr. Bleakman says—before he realizes that sharing the park with dogs is much more fun.

An Itchy Day: Clifford has an itchy patch! He's afraid to go to the vet, so he tries to hide his scratching from Emily Elizabeth. But Clifford soon realizes that it's better to be truthful and trust the person he loves most— Emily Elizabeth.

The Doggy Detectives: Oh, no! Emily Elizabeth is accused of stealing Jetta's gold medal—and then her shiny mirror! But her dear Clifford never doubts her innocence and, with his fellow doggy detectives, finds the real thief.

Follow the Leader: While playing follow-the-leader with Clifford and T-Bone, Cleo learns that playing fair is the best way to play!

The Big Red Mess: Clifford tries to stay clean for the Dog of the Year contest, but he ends up becoming a big red mess! However, when Clifford helps the judge reach the shore safely, he finds that he doesn't need to stay clean to be the Dog of the Year.

The Big Surprise: Poor Clifford. It's his birthday, but none of his friends will play with him. Maybe it's because they're all busy. . . planning his surprise party!

The Wild Ice Cream Machine: Charley and Emily Elizabeth decide to work the ice cream machine themselves. Things go smoothly. . . until the lever gets stuck and they find themselves knee-deep in ice cream!

Dogs and Cats: Can dogs and cats be friends? Clifford, T-Bone, and Cleo don't think so. But they have a change of heart after they help two lost kittens find their mother.

The Magic Ball: Emily Elizabeth trusts Clifford to deliver a package to the post office, but he opens it and breaks the gift inside. Clifford tries to hide his blunder, but Emily Elizabeth appreciates honesty and understands that accidents happen.